For Nusayba, Hanifa, Anisa, Zineera, and anyone
who has ever felt misunderstood . . . —R.F.

For all the children who might need a little help
speaking up for themselves. —A.B.

Library of Congress Control Number: 2023943302
ISBN 978-0-06-320618-2

The artist used Procreate and Adobe Photoshop to create
the digital illustrations for this book.
Typography by Cara Llewellyn

24 25 26 27 28 RTLO 10 9 8 7 6 5 4 3 2 1
First Edition

Do You Even Know Me?

Illustrated by
ANI BUSHRY

Written by
REEM FARUQI

My crayons are extra wobbly today.
I don't like the news on TV.

My ears hear the word *Muslim* over and over.
When the reporter says the words,
her eyebrows go down and her mouth frowns.

I am Muslim.

My name is Salma, which means peace.
Islam also means peace.
I wish more people knew that.

I make sure my big sister and
little brother share their candy.

I never step on ants on purpose.

I never push in the lunch line.

Skye is my
best friend.

We do everything
together.

But today, at school, she is absent.

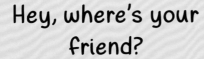

Hey, where's your friend?

Probably no one will ever sit with you or your people anymore.

My cheeks flush.

I open my mouth to answer, but Luke has already walked away.

My sandwich doesn't taste good anymore.

On the playground, Luke bumps into me.
I drop my jump rope.

He smiles.

How can a smile make me feel so bad?

Ms. Lin reads us a book about bullies.
Skye nudges me.
I look down at the rug.
When I look up, Luke is staring at me.

Ms. Lin picks Luke to
pass out pencils.
She smiles at him.

I want to tell Ms. Lin,
but I don't know how to tell her.
I don't know *what* to tell her.

Luke grabs my library book.
My skin feels hot.

He shoves it back on the shelf
and pushes past me.

I don't like how I feel
when Luke picks on me.

I don't like how I
feel when I don't say
anything about it.

I don't like how I feel
when I don't *do* anything.

I take a deep breath.

I ball my fists.

I raise my chin.

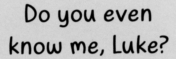

Do you even know me, Luke?

The lunch table gets quiet.

I know all about Muzzzlims from TV!

I'm Muslim.

The *s* makes my
voice soft.

My name and my religion
mean peace.

What you see on TV
is not who I am.

Skye holds my hand.
I feel brave.
I tell Ms. Lin everything.

Luke gets Silent Lunch and no recess.

The next day
Luke doesn't
look at me.

He doesn't bother me
during story time.

Or at the playground.

Or at lunch.

One day Luke passes
the ball to me.
I score a goal.

Luke tries to high-five me.
I don't high-five him back.

You were mean to me
and I didn't like it.

Sorry...

This time he looks like he means it.

One day at lunch Luke's best friend is absent.

I remember how that felt.

I remember the meaning of my name.

I take a deep breath.

Want to eat lunch with us?

AUTHOR'S NOTE

I wrote this story after former president Donald Trump enforced the Muslim Ban throughout the United States in 2017. Hearing the word Muslim over and over on television made me feel wobbly inside. I didn't like how Muslim was mispronounced and wasn't said in a kind voice. Later, in 2021, President Joe Biden reversed the Muslim Ban, but there is still much work to be done. I hope and pray that no matter what faith you are, you are accepted and know that you are welcome anywhere you choose to be.

ILLUSTRATOR'S NOTE

I think creating a tolerant and accepting society begins with us as individuals. And an integral part of that starts with acceptance of people of different faiths. No one should be bullied for their faith. And by being wary of misinformation and stereotyping, we can avoid contributing to discrimination and divisiveness. By being accepting of each other, we can find strength in our differences.

www.thefyi.org/toolkits/youth-support-tool-kit

www.isbatlanta.org/wp-content/uploads/2023/08/ISB_Bullying2023.pdf

www.stopbullying.gov

ing.org/resources/for-students/anti-bullying-resources/bullying-prevention-guide

www.jacksoncountycombat.com/300/Who-Is-At-Risk

www.ispu.org/american-muslim-poll-2022-1

www.adl.org/sites/default/files/10-Ways-to-Respond-to-Bullying.pdf

www.onoursleeves.org/mental-health-resources/articles-support/bullying/bullying-affects-everyone